Monica

and the

Weekend

of Drama

by Diana G. Gallagher

E 50

77

STONE ARCH BOOKS
a capstone imprint

Monica is published by Stone Arch Books
A Capstone Imprint
151 Good Counsel Drive, P.O. Box 669
Mankato, Minnesota 56002
www.capstonepub.com

Printed in the United States of America in Stevens Point, Wisconsin.
032011
006111WZF11

Library of Congress Cataloging-in-Publication Data
Gallagher, Diana G.
  Monica and the weekend of drama / by Diana G. Gallagher.
    p. cm.
  Summary: When her mother cannot find a babysitter for the weekend, thirteen-year-old Monica is left in charge of the house and her stepsister Angela, with disastrous results.
  ISBN-13: 978-1-4342-2557-3 (library binding)
  ISBN-10: 1-4342-2557-7 (library binding)
  1. Responsibility--Juvenile fiction. 2. Self-reliance--Juvenile fiction.
3. Babysitters--Juvenile fiction. 4. Stepsisters--Juvenile fiction. 5.
Emergencies--Juvenile fiction. [1. Responsiblity--Fiction. 2. Self-reliance
--Fiction. 3. Babysitters--Fiction. 4. Stepsisters--Fiction. 5. Emergencies--
Fiction.] I. Title.
  PZ7.G13543Mpt 2011
  813.54--dc22   2011001992

Art Director/Graphic Designer: Kay Fraser
Production Specialist: Michelle Biedscheid

Photo credits:
Cover: Delaney Photography
Avatars: Delaney Photography (Claudia), Shutterstock: Aija Avotina (guitar), Alex Staroseltsev (baseball), Andrii Muzyka (bowling ball), Anton9 (reptile), bsites (hat), debra hughes (tree), Dietmar Höpfl (lightning), Dr_Flash (Earth), Elaine Barker (star), Ivelin Radkov (money), Michael D Brown (smiley face), Mikhail (horse), originalpunkt (paintbrushes), pixel-pets (dog), R. Gino Santa Maria (football), Ruth Black (cupcake), Shvaygert Ekaterina (horseshoe), SPYDER (crown), Tischenko Irina (flower), VectorZilla (clown), Volkova Anna (heart); Capstone Studio: Karon Dubke (horse Monica, horse Chloe)

-----------------------{ table of contents }-----------------------

WELCOME BACK, MONICA MURRAY   SCREEN NAME: MonicaLuvsHorses

 YOUR AVATAR PICTURE

All updates from your friends

 TRACI GREGORY I can't wait for my vacation with Logan Gregory! A whole weekend at Lost Lagoon with my sweetie.

 Logan Gregory | I can't wait either!

 Frank Jones | Uh oh. I can't be home during the day this weekend. My friend is sick.

 Traci Gregory | Dad! You promised! We'll have to talk about this tonight.

 Monica Murray | I can handle it! Don't worry about it, Mom!

 Traci Gregory | Like I said, we'll have to talk about this tonight. Monica, you're not old enough.

 MONICA MURRAY is NOT a little kid.
Claudia Cortez and 6 other people like this.

 RORY WEBER has sooooo much homework. Guess I know what I'm doing this weekend when I'm not working. :(

 CLAUDIA CORTEZ Has anyone seen Music Mania? It's the DVD I'm getting next and I wanted to know what people thought.

 Brad Turino | I loved it. I'd watch it again.

 Adam Locke | Me too, it was so good!

 Monica Murray | I haven't seen it. Maybe we can watch it this weekend???

 Becca McDougal | Me either. I heard it was really good, though.

FRANK JONES I'm thinking about my friend George Fenton. He's not doing well right now. Glad he has a great daughter to help him out, and glad I can be there for him this weekend.

 Monica Murray   Sorry about your friend, Grandpa!

 Frank Jones   Thanks, honey.

 CHLOE GRANGER Is it Friday yet????

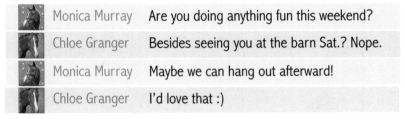

Monica Murray   Are you doing anything fun this weekend?

Chloe Granger   Besides seeing you at the barn Sat.? Nope.

Monica Murray   Maybe we can hang out afterward!

Chloe Granger   I'd love that :)

 MONICA MURRAY to BECCA MCDOUGAL want to hang out Friday night?

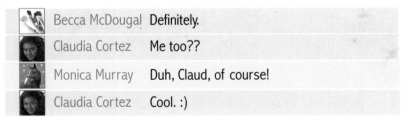

Becca McDougal   Definitely.

Claudia Cortez   Me too??

Monica Murray   Duh, Claud, of course!

Claudia Cortez   Cool. :)

 ANGELA GREGORY has updated her interests. She added "Playing with dolls" to her favorite activities.

Chapter One

On My Own

❖ I had some freedom.

I could go to the mall and the movies with my friends, and I usually rode my bike to the barn where I took riding lessons. I walked to school by myself or with my friends every day. I could stay out until eleven, except for school nights. I was thirteen, not four years old.

But my mom didn't think I was old enough to stay home alone — during the day — for two days!

I wasn't supposed to know that. I found out when I overheard heard Mom talking to Grandpa in the kitchen one day.

"Logan and I made reservations at Lost Lagoon three months ago," Mom said. "You promised you'd be around to take care of Angela and Monica. I need you here for the girls this weekend, Dad."

"My friend George Fenton needs me more," Grandpa said. "He's really sick."

"Wait a second. George Fenton's daughter is a nurse, isn't she?" Mom said. "Why can't she take care of her dad?"

"Doreen is working double shifts at the hospital all week. Staffing problems," Grandpa explained. "I'll be home by 9:30, Traci. Monica and Angela won't be alone at night."

"I can't leave them alone during the day either," Mom said.

That's when I rushed through the kitchen door. "I'm home alone after school all the time," I said. "I can handle things for two days."

Angela came stomping in from the backyard. "No way. What if you burn the pizza again?" she said. "And there's smoke everywhere and the alarm goes off. Brrrrrt. Brrrrrt! And Buttons starts howling 'cause she doesn't like the noise."

"That's not going to happen," I said, glaring at Angela.

"Monica. When did that happen?" Mom asked, narrowing her eyes.

"The last time Monica watched me," Angela said.

"I opened a window and turned on the fan and the alarm shut off," I said. "There wasn't a fire or anything."

"The pizza burned," Angela said.

"It wasn't burned," I said. "It was just a little black on the bottom."

"I want an adult to be here," Mom said.

"Mom, seriously, I can handle it!" I protested.

"I'm calling Mrs. Addison," Mom said.

"No!" Angela whined. "I don't want the stinky lady!"

Mrs. Addison watched Angela when everyone else was busy. She was a very nice old lady, but she wore super strong, super stinky perfume. She also had peppermint breath.

Mom flipped open her phone and started dialing. I threw my hands up and went into my own room.

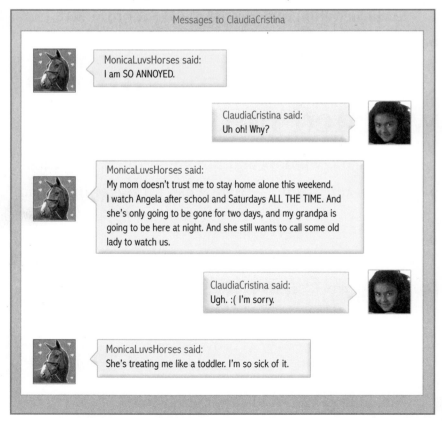

Messages to ClaudiaCristina

MonicaLuvsHorses said:
I am SO ANNOYED.

ClaudiaCristina said:
Uh oh! Why?

MonicaLuvsHorses said:
My mom doesn't trust me to stay home alone this weekend. I watch Angela after school and Saturdays ALL THE TIME. And she's only going to be gone for two days, and my grandpa is going to be here at night. And she still wants to call some old lady to watch us.

ClaudiaCristina said:
Ugh. :(I'm sorry.

MonicaLuvsHorses said:
She's treating me like a toddler. I'm so sick of it.

"Monica!" Mom called. She knocked on my door and then came in before I answered. "Mrs. Addison is busy this weekend."

I sat up.

"And I can't find anyone else on such short notice," Mom went on.

"So does that mean you're staying home?" I asked.

"No," Mom said. "Reservations at Lost Lagoon are too hard to get. Besides, we already paid for the first night."

"Then what's going to happen?" I asked.

Mom sighed. "You'll be in charge while Grandpa is with Mr. Fenton," she said.

I almost shrieked for joy. But I wanted to act like an adult, so instead, I just nodded. "Don't worry, Mom. We'll be fine," I said.

"I know," Mom said. "But if something goes wrong and you can't get Grandpa, you can call Becca's mom and dad."

The McDougals lived next door. Becca was my next best friend after Claudia.

"I will," I said.

Chapter Two

Stuck
With Nick

Mom and Logan left early Friday afternoon. After school, Claudia and Becca went with me to pick up Angela at the elementary school. We waited near the front door so she couldn't miss us.

Claudia's neighbor, Mrs. Wright, couldn't miss us either.

"Claudia!" Mrs. Wright yelled as she walked toward us. Her bratty son, Nick, was digging in his heels. She had to drag him behind her. I cringed as soon as I saw Nick.

"Hi, Mrs. Wright," Claudia said.

"I need a huge favor," Mrs. Wright said.

Watching Nick was the only favor Mrs. Wright ever wanted. Claudia was stuck babysitting her terror-tot neighbor more often than I had to watch my sister.

"Nick hates grocery shopping," Mrs. Wright explained. "He always misbehaves when I take him."

Nick acted up no matter where he was or what he was doing. He threw temper tantrums constantly. But he could be bribed.

"Buy him donuts or ice cream," Becca said.

"Or promise to take him to the park," I said.

"He never turns down money," Claudia added.

"Except in the grocery store," Mrs. Wright said. "He hates grocery shopping. I don't get it."

"The store smells funny, and it's too cold," Nick whined. His whole body went limp. His mother let go and he plopped on the ground.

Angela ran over. "Why are you sitting in the dirt, Nick?" she yelled.

"I like dirt," Nick said.

"Please, Claudia?" Mrs. Wright asked. She held out $20.

Claudia sighed. But she took the money. As soon as she did, Nick's mom hurried toward her car. I knew she wanted to get away before Claudia could change her mind.

Nick stood up. "Can we go to the park?" he asked.

"I want to go to the park, too! Can we go, Monica?" Angela squealed.

"I didn't ask you," Nick said.

Angela put her hands on her hips. "I can go to the park if I want to," she growled.

"Stop it!" Claudia snapped. "Nobody's going to the park. We're all going home."

"Okay," Angela said. She edged closer to Nick and added, "We can walk together."

"I'm not walking with a stupid girl!" Nick screamed. He marched ahead. Angela ran to catch up. That just made Nick walk faster.

I didn't feel like breaking up fights or chasing two elementary school kids down the street.

"I bet you guys can't be totally silent for five minutes," I said, winking at my friends.

"I don't want to," Nick said.

"Because you can't," Angela said.

Nick glared at her. "I can too," he said.

"Prove it!" Angela dared him.

I looked at my phone to check the time. "Starting in three, two, one — now!" I yelled.

Both kids pressed their lips together and started walking.

"That was brilliant," Claudia whispered.

"Or lucky," I said. "The weekend just started. I've got two days and five hours to go."

"It's so cool that your parents left you in charge," Becca said.

"Yeah," Claudia said. "My brother is always home when my parents go away. I take care of myself, but I never get credit for it."

"Neither do I!" Becca exclaimed.

"You're an only child," Claudia said.

"I stay alone after school," Becca said, "but my parents always take me on their weekend getaways."

"I wish Daddy would take me!" Angela shouted.

"I win!" Nick said. He laughed. "You talked and the five minutes aren't up!"

"So?" Angela asked. She gave him the hands-on-hips stare again. "I don't care."

Nick grinned and said, "You're just mad because you lost."

Angela narrowed her eyes. "No," she said. "I'm mad because I have to spend two whole days with Monica."

"What's wrong with that?" Becca asked.

"She's boring," Angela replied, "and she's bossy." She stuck out her lip and scowled.

My sister is a nightmare when she's mad or bored.
I had to keep her happy or the weekend would be a
disaster!

"I was going to make cookies and watch Princess
Patsy and go to the park, but if you think that's boring,
we can just sit in the living room and wait for Mom and
Logan to get back," I said.

"Princess Patsy!" Nick yelled. "Gross." He stuck his
finger in his mouth and pretended to gag.

"I'm getting cookies and going to the park and you're
not!" Angela yelled, sticking out her tongue.

Claudia rolled her eyes. "I'm getting *Music Mania* in
the mail today," she said. "Maybe we can all watch it
this weekend. But not at my house. Mom is cleaning the
carpets or something."

"We could watch it at my house," Becca said. "But
my mom will want to watch it with us."

Becca's mother was nice, but she hovered.

"Let's watch it at my house," I said.

"Fantastic!" Claudia said. She grinned.

"I'll be there," Becca said.

"What about Princess Patsy?" Angela asked.

"We'll watch cartoons in the morning and the movie in the afternoon," I said. "It's a funny movie. You'll like it."

"Can Nick come?" Angela asked.

At the same time, Becca, Claudia, and I said, "No!"

Chapter Three

In Case of
Emergencies

Angela bugged me all the way home. "Why can't Nick come?" she kept saying. "This isn't Claudia's house. She can't make the rules."

As soon as we walked in the house, she stomped into the kitchen and dropped her backpack on the floor.

"It's not fair," she yelled.

My stepsister was like monster glue. Once she got stuck on something, she stayed stuck. She would keep asking, pouting, and stomping until I gave in — or outsmarted her.

"Nick can't come because he's a boy," I said.

"So?" Angela asked, looking puzzled.

"So we have a no-boys rule," I said. "No boys allowed when Logan and Mom aren't home. Seriously. Mom said."

Angela frowned. "Are you sure?" she asked suspiciously.

"Positive," I said.

That wasn't exactly a lie. But it wasn't the truth, either.

Mom and Logan never actually said that I couldn't have boys over when they weren't home. I wasn't sure why, since it was a rule for most of my friends.

Maybe my mom thought I wasn't old enough to like boys so I didn't need a no-boys rule — yet. The more I thought about it, I started to get kind of annoyed. Why didn't I have a no-boys rule?

But it didn't matter as long as Angela thought we had a rule.

"Rats!" Angela yelled. She kicked a chair.

PineTreeMom said:
Call Grandpa if you go anywhere.

MonicaLuvsHorses said:
Okay, Mom. Have fun!

PineTreeMom said:
And don't tell anyone you're home alone.

MonicaLuvsHorses said:
Got it, Mom. Don't worry.

PineTreeMom said:
I left $50 for you on the kitchen table.

ANGELATHEANGEL said:
Can we buy Princess Patsy stuff on ebay???

PineTreeMom said:
No! It's for food. And emergencies.

PineTreeMom said:
NOT that there should be any emergencies!

PineTreeMom said:
Grandpa said he'd buy mac and cheese for dinner.

MonicaLuvsHorses said:
Mom! I can handle it! Have fun.

Angela looked nervous. "What if something awful happens while Traci and Daddy are gone?" she asked me.

"Nothing's going to happen," I said.

"It might," Angela said.

"Then I'll call Becca's dad," I told her.

"What if he isn't home?" Angela asked.

"Then I'll call 911," I said.

"What if they don't answer?" Angela asked. She started to look really panicked.

I rolled my eyes. "Angela. It's 911," I said. "They always answer."

"Okay," she said. But she still looked pretty nervous.

Just then, I heard whining. Buttons was standing by the back door. I gave Angela some cookies and sent her outside to play with the dog. I wanted to get my homework done. Then I could enjoy the rest of the weekend.

After I'd been working for a while, I started to get hungry. There wasn't much to eat in the fridge, though. And Mom had said there would be mac and cheese, but I couldn't find any.

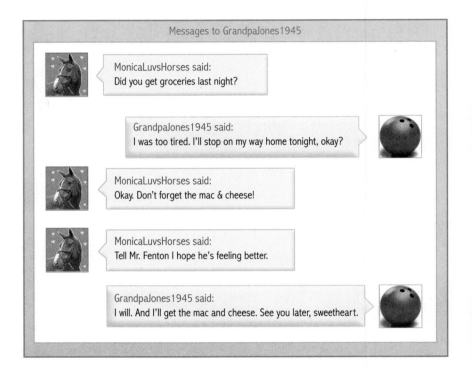

Angela came back inside at 6:12.

"Are you hungry?" I asked.

"I'm starving," she said. "I want mac and cheese."

Ugh. This wasn't going to be good.

"Grandpa didn't go to the store," I said. "We can have mac and cheese tomorrow."

"Why didn't he go?" Angela asked.

"I don't know," I said. "I guess he was too tired after helping Mr. Fenton all day."

Angela stomped her foot. "He should help US!" she screeched. "Not some old guy."

I laughed. "That old guy is one of Grandpa's best friends," I told her. "Anyway, Grandpa does help us. Every day. But today we can't have mac and cheese, because we don't have any."

"The stinky lady doesn't make it from a box," Angela said. "She scratches it."

"You mean she makes it from scratch," I said. "Well, sorry, but I don't know how to do that."

"We're gonna starve to death!" Angela wailed. "I knew my dad shouldn't go away and leave me with you!"

"We won't starve," I said. "We've got lots of stuff to eat."

Angela sniffled. "Like what?" she asked.

I looked through the cupboard and pulled out a can of soup. "You love chicken noodle soup with crackers!" I said.

"I had that yesterday," Angela said.

There was a loaf of bread on the counter. "Peanut butter and jelly?" I asked.

"I hate peanut butter and jelly," Angela said. She made a face.

I spotted a box of cereal on top of the fridge. "I know you like Apple-Os," I said.

"I like Apple-Os for *breakfast*," Angela said. Then she ran out of the room crying.

I didn't want cereal either. I opened the freezer again. All we had was frozen peas, sausage, and fish cakes.

And $50.00.

I picked up the phone to order pizza, but instead of a dial tone, I heard a voice.

Angela was using the phone in the living room.

"911," a woman said. "What is your emergency?"

"My sister won't feed me!" Angela sobbed.

My heart jumped into my throat.

Calling 911 for something stupid was a crime! Did they send little kids to jail? Or lock up the person who was supposed to be watching them?

Chapter Four

Texting While Babysitting

"It's against the law to prank-call 911, young lady," the 911 woman said sternly.

I knew I had to do something. "Um, hi," I said. I was nervous, and my voice shook. "She called when I wasn't looking. We don't have an emergency."

"Yes, we do!" Angela exclaimed. "I'm hungry!"

"I picked up the phone to order a pizza," I said.

"You didn't tell me that!" Angela yelled happily. She hung up.

"I'm really sorry," I told the 911 responder. "It won't happen again."

"I'll let it go," the woman said.

"Thanks," I said. That was a huge relief.

Angela marched into the kitchen. "I want pepperoni," she said. "That's it. No onions and no green peppers."

"Promise you won't call 911 again," I said.

"What if the house is on fire and you're asleep and I can't wake you up?" Angela asked.

"Then you can call 911," I said.

"Okay," Angela said. "I'm gonna watch TV."

I ordered the pizza. Then I took paper plates and napkins into the living room. Angela was sprawled on the floor watching Baby Brats cartoons.

Messages to Horses4Chloe

MonicaLuvsHorses said:
Hey! What's up?

"We can't eat in the living room," Angela said.

"I'm in charge tonight, and I say it's okay," I told her. I reached for the remote and scanned through the program guide. "But I'm tired of cartoons. Let's find something else."

"I like cartoons," Angela said.

"Let's watch a movie," I suggested. I found one I wanted to see and changed the channel. It was a horror movie called *Monsters of Hollow High*, and it was supposed to be absolutely terrible in a hilarious way.

"I'm not supposed to watch scary stuff," Angela said. She sat down next to me on the couch.

"This one is so cheesy it's funny," I told her. I took a bite of pizza and settled back.

Messages to MonicaLuvsHorses

Horses4Chloe said:
I think Cameron likes someone else. Can you call me????

MonicaLuvsHorses said:
OMG. I will. As soon as Angela goes to bed.

Soon, Angela was totally into the movie. "That girl was mean to the muddy monster kid," Angela said, pointing at the screen. "I think he's going to get her in the bathtub."

Two minutes later the mud guy oozed out of the bathtub drain. He scared the mean girl, but she screamed and got away.

Angela watched the rest of the movie through her fingers. She was being good, so I let her stay up late to see the end. I didn't even yell when she fed pizza crusts to Buttons.

"I don't want a bath," Angela said when the movie was done.

Angela usually had to take a bath every night, but she didn't look dirty. And I wanted her to go to bed so I could talk to Chloe about the Cameron crisis.

Cameron wasn't exactly Chloe's boyfriend, but they liked each other. So if he liked someone else, Chloe would be devastated.

"Okay, but you'll have to take a bath tomorrow," I said.

I tucked Angela in with her favorite stuffed animals. I left the nightlight on and the door open.

Before I'd even made it back into the living room to call Chloe, I heard a scream.

I rushed back to Angela's room. She was hiding under the covers.

"What's the matter?" I asked.

"The mud man is going to get me," Angela said.

"There's no such thing as a mud man," I said. I sat on the edge of her bed. "It was just a movie. It's not real."

Angela pushed the covers down. Her cheeks were streaked with tears. She wasn't faking. She was really scared.

"I know it's not real," she said. "But the scary pictures are in my head. Will you read me a story?"

I picked up the book on her nightstand and started reading *Lucy Blue's Picnic Surprise*.

"Lucy Blue wanted to do something special for her friend, Samantha . . ." I began. I used different voices for all the characters.

Angela giggled once while I read. She even yawned.

Finally, I got to the last page. "Lucy had a wonderful day, but she was so tired she fell asleep before her head hit the pillow. The end." I put the book down and smiled. "All better now?" I asked.

Angela squeezed her eyes closed for three seconds. "No," she whispered. "The mud guy is still there."

I glanced at the clock. If Angela didn't fall asleep soon, it would be too late to call Chloe.

"Maybe music will help," I suggested. I put a CD in her CD player. Then I started to leave the room.

"Don't leave me!" Angela wailed. She closed her eyes when I sat down.

I waited three minutes, and then tried to sneak out. She grabbed my hand. I couldn't leave.

I was still sitting with her when Grandpa came home at 10:30.

"Monica?" Grandpa called out softly. He frowned when he found me in Angela's room. "Is Angela okay?" he asked.

"She can't sleep," I said.

"Too much junk food?" Grandpa asked.

"I'm scared of the mud man in the movie," Angela said.

"The mud man? What movie?" Grandpa asked. He sounded tired.

"The monster movie I watched with Monica," Angela said.

"You let her watch a monster movie?" Grandpa asked angrily. "I thought you had more sense than that, Monica."

"It wasn't that scary," I said. "I thought it was funny."

"You're thirteen. Angela is only eight," Grandpa said. He looked at his watch. "I'm going to call Mrs. Addison to come over tomorrow."

"No stinky lady!" Angela yelled. "I'll go to sleep right now." She pulled the covers over her head.

"I'm sorry, Grandpa," I said. "Please, give me another chance."

Grandpa sighed. "Okay," he said. "I'm too tired to argue, and I've got to get up early. I'm going to bed."

I waited until I heard Grandpa's bedroom door close. When I started to leave, I heard Angela sniffle.

Messages to MonicaLuvsHorses

MonicaLuvsHorses said:
I can't call you tonight. A. won't go to sleep. I'm sorry.

Horses4Chloe said:
That's okay. We can talk at the barn tomorrow. I'll watch her while you ride.

"Are you still scared?" I asked.

She poked her head out and nodded. I sat down.

I stretched out next to Angela. I knew she'd fall asleep soon. But fixing things with Grandpa might not be so easy. He was worried about his sick friend, and I had let him down. I felt awful.

I made a vow to get through the rest of the weekend without making any more mistakes.

Chapter Five

Questions
About Boys

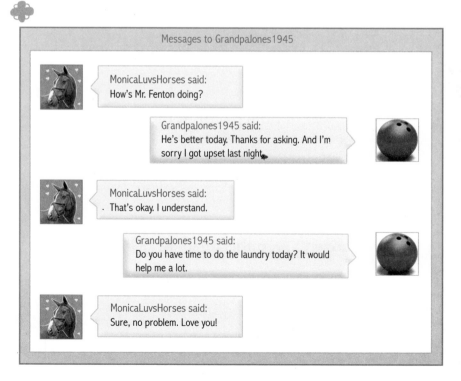

Messages to GrandpaJones1945

MonicaLuvsHorses said:
How's Mr. Fenton doing?

GrandpaJones1945 said:
He's better today. Thanks for asking. And I'm sorry I got upset last night.

MonicaLuvsHorses said:
. That's okay. I understand.

GrandpaJones1945 said:
Do you have time to do the laundry today? It would help me a lot.

MonicaLuvsHorses said:
Sure, no problem. Love you!

When she woke up on Saturday morning, Angela ate Apple-Os and watched Princess Patsy cartoons.

Grandpa usually did the laundry when Mom worked. I didn't mind helping him out. I put a load of dirty clothes in the washer.

Then I remembered that I'd promised Angela I'd make cookies. I found an easy cookie recipe online. You didn't even have to use the oven. The cookies baked in the microwave. When I checked the cupboards, I saw that we had all of the ingredients except cocoa and quick oats.

I put the breakfast dishes in the sink. "Angela!" I called.

"What?" Angela hollered from the living room.

"I need your help!" I said. I rinsed the dishes and put them in the dishwasher. Then I dragged my sister away from the TV.

"Hey! I haven't seen this one!" Angela exclaimed.

"You can watch it later," I said. "We have to pick up before we leave for my riding lesson."

"Why?" Angela asked. "Nobody's going to make us clean up."

I wanted to prove I was responsible and dependable. And I wanted the house to look nice when Becca and Claudia came over. But those reasons wouldn't convince Angela.

"Mom and Logan will yell if they come home to a mess," I said. "We might even get grounded."

Angela shrugged. "I don't care," she said.

"Okay," I said. "If we don't do the chores, we can't go to the barn."

I didn't mean it. I absolutely had to go. I needed to talk to Chloe.

"Can we go to the park?" Angela asked.

"Maybe tomorrow," I said. "Claudia and Becca are coming over today, remember?"

Angela frowned. "Can we still make cookies?" she asked.

"If I don't miss my riding lesson," I said. I put our used paper plates and napkins in the pizza box.

Angela sighed. "What do you want me to do?" she asked.

Angela took out the garbage. I vacuumed up pizza crumbs and started another load of laundry. Then I changed into my riding clothes and hustled Angela out the door.

We got to the stable a few minutes early. Chloe was sitting on the front bench.

"I told Rory that you and I had to talk," Chloe said. "He's getting Lancelot ready for you."

"Is Megan here?" Angela asked.

"She's in the tack room," Chloe said.

Megan Fitch was a rich, snotty kid who owned a fancy show horse. Chloe owned a show horse too, but she wasn't bossy, mean, or stuck up.

Megan had one thing in her favor, though. She treated Angela like a princess, and Angela adored her. So I guess she wasn't all bad.

After Angela left I sat down next to Chloe. "So what's up with Cameron?" I asked.

Chloe sighed. "I'm not sure," she said. "He still talks to me, but not like he used to. **Not like he really likes me.**"

"I bet he doesn't want to let you know he really likes you in case you don't really like him back," I said. I knew what I was talking about. That's how I was around Rory.

"I don't think so," Chloe said. "Not anymore. He ate lunch with Katy Connor four times last week. And I saw them walking home together. Twice!"

"Maybe they're partners on a project," I said.

Chloe shook her head. "I have all the same classes as both of them," she said. "We don't have a big project right now."

"Things aren't always what they seem," I said. "Hanging out doesn't have to be romantic. I bet there's another explanation."

"Maybe, but I'm not going to ask," Chloe said.

Chloe couldn't ask, but I could try to find out. "Claudia and Becca are coming over to watch Music Mania this afternoon," I said. "You should come too."

"Mom is taking me to the mall," Chloe said.

"She can bring you to my house when you're done," I said. "We won't start the movie until you get there."

"Okay," Chloe said. "I haven't seen Music Mania."

Just then, Rory walked out of the barn with Lancelot. "I haven't seen it, either, but I heard it's really funny," he said.

"Yeah, I could use a good laugh," Chloe said.

It seemed like Rory wanted to come too. But I didn't want to ask him. I didn't want him to feel out of place with so many girls.

And I didn't want to ask him and risk him saying no.

Chapter Six

Grocery
Problems

Angela and I went to the grocery store after my lesson. Besides the cookie ingredients, I decided to get some chips and salsa, plus drinks for everyone to have while we watched the movie. There wasn't much else to eat in our house.

"Can I get fruit cocktail and sherbet?" Angela asked. "And some funny face cookies from the bakery?"

"We don't have enough money," I said.

Angela gasped. "Did you lose our fifty dollars?" she whispered.

"No, I bought pizza," I said. "That was eleven dollars with the tip, and I need party snacks. We can't spend it all."

Angela's eyes narrowed. "Grandpa will be mad if you feed your friends and you don't feed me," she said.

I didn't want any more trouble with Grandpa, so I put fruit cocktail and sherbet in our cart. I also bought popcorn, and veggies and dip.

I spent a total of $24.73. That meant I only had $14.27 left.

I crossed my fingers and hoped we didn't have a real emergency. I didn't want to have to use my savings if something went wrong. I was saving that money for new riding boots.

We got home forty-five minutes before Claudia and Becca were due to arrive. That was plenty of time to cut up the veggies and make cookies. But first, I had to invite Cameron.

I reached for my phone, but it wasn't in my pocket. "I lost my phone!" I shrieked.

"No, you didn't," Angela said. "It's right there." She pointed at the counter.

My cell phone was lying on the counter. I had left for the barn in such a hurry I forgot it.

My relief didn't last long. I hadn't missed any important texts from my friends. But I had three new voicemails.

And all three of them were from Grandpa.

He left the first message during my riding lesson. He left the second an hour later, when he called and couldn't get me. And the third message was from five minutes ago.

I called him back, hoping he wasn't too mad.

"Where have you been?" Grandpa asked.

"At my riding lesson," I began. "Then we—"

Grandpa didn't let me finish. He yelled into the phone, "I called the barn. You left over an hour ago!"

"We stopped at the store," I said.

"Why didn't you call to let me know?" Grandpa asked. "I've been worried sick."

"I forgot to take my phone," I said. "I'm sorry."

I couldn't believe it. I had let my grandfather down again!

Chapter Seven

What
No-Boys Rule?

Messages to NoStrikesCameron

MonicaLuvsHorses said:
A bunch of us are watching Music Mania at my house today. Want to come?

NoStrikesCameron said:
I already saw it. But who's going to be there?

MonicaLuvsHorses said:
A couple of my Pine Tree friends. And Chloe, of course.

NoStrikesCameron said:
I'll be there. What time?

MonicaLuvsHorses said:
3. See you later. :)

The Princess Patsy theme song blared from the living room. I rushed back into the kitchen to cut up carrots. I was mixing cookie dough when Claudia and Becca rang the doorbell.

"We can't watch the movie now," Angela said. "Monica hasn't finished the cookies yet."

"That's fine with us," Becca said. "We don't want to start until Tommy and Adam get here."

"And maybe Brad," Claudia added. "If Adam took the hint and asked him."

"I didn't know you asked the guys to come," I said nervously, glancing at Angela. Would she remember the no-boys rule I'd made up?

"They can't come," Angela said. "They're boys!"

Oh, no. I had to think fast. "I'm in charge, so we don't have a no-boys rule today," I said.

I was pretty sure Mom wouldn't exactly approve, but Claudia had a crush on Brad, and Becca really liked Tommy. I didn't want to ruin their afternoon.

Besides, I had just invited Cameron.

"Then I want Nick to come," Angela said.

"No!" Claudia, Becca, and I answered at the same time.

"I want to be able to relax and watch the movie," Claudia said. "There's no way that would happen with Nick around. Sorry, Angela."

"That's not fair!" Angela yelled. She stuck out her lip and folded her arms.

Claudia and Becca looked at me. They knew that Angela shrieked and stomped and made things horrible when she was mad.

"Maybe we can meet Claudia and Nick at the park one day next week," I suggested. I dropped spoonfuls of dough on a plate.

"We can do that," Claudia said.

"With ice cream," Angela said.

"Deal," Claudia said. She and Angela shook on it. Then the doorbell rang.

Claudia, Becca, and Angela left to answer the door.

I put the first batch of cookies in the microwave and set the timer. I heard boys' voices coming from the living room.

Adam, Tommy, Brad, and Cameron had arrived at the same time. Adam and Brad knew Cameron from baseball. Pine Tree and Rock Creek played against each other a lot.

Chloe was late. And Cameron didn't ask about her.

That wasn't good.

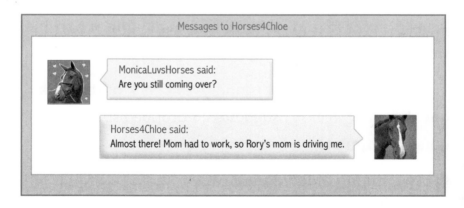

Messages to Horses4Chloe

MonicaLuvsHorses said:
Are you still coming over?

Horses4Chloe said:
Almost there! Mom had to work, so Rory's mom is driving me.

Rory!

I should have invited him that morning at the barn. Now I had a second chance.

I went outside and waited.

When Mrs. Weber stopped at the curb, I ran to the car. Rory was sitting in the passenger seat. He rolled down his window.

"Do you want to watch the movie with us, Rory?" I asked.

"Yeah!" Rory said. He grinned. "Thanks."

Chloe looked at me. "Who's here?" she asked.

"Claudia, Becca, Adam, Brad, Tommy . . . and Cameron," I said. I winked. She got a huge smile on her face. Then the three of us headed up the sidewalk.

Everything was working out great. Until we walked into the house. Right away, we got clobbered by flying cookies.

"Sorry!" Adam said when he saw me. He caught the cookie Tommy threw at him.

"What's going on?" I asked.

I picked up two cookies from the floor. They were hard as rocks. Bits had broken off when they hit the floor.

"Angela thought the cookies were too mushy or something," Becca explained. "So she cooked them for five more minutes."

"And made throwing disks!" Claudia added. She squealed and hid behind Brad.

Angela was under the hall table, giggling, as cookies flew in all directions. Buttons was hiding next to her. The poor dog didn't seem to think it was funny.

"Look out, Chloe!" Cameron called.

Chloe moved the wrong way, and the cookie hit her arm. "Ouch!" she yelled.

Cameron rushed to her side. "Are you okay?" he asked. "I'm really sorry. I didn't mean to hit you."

Chloe rubbed her arm and smiled. "I'm fine," she said.

I wasn't fine. I was annoyed.

The hall and living room were covered with crumbs. I knew I wouldn't be able to clean up until everyone left. But I had to stop the cookie fight before something got broken.

"Let's watch the movie!" I said. "Popcorn and fruit punch coming right up!"

"Fantastic," Adam said, flopping on the floor in front of the TV. "I'm thirsty."

Angela followed me into the kitchen. "Are you going to make cookies I can eat?" she asked.

I knew the cookies I'd already made would have been good if she hadn't overcooked them, but I held my tongue. "As soon as I get popcorn and drinks," I said.

"Okay," she said. Then she ran back to the living room.

I microwaved two bags of popcorn and counted out paper cups. I put the cups on a tray and poured punch into them. I carried the popcorn out first.

Angela was sitting with Adam, Claudia, and Brad on the floor. Becca and Tommy were squeezed into Logan's recliner. Rory, Chloe, and Cameron were sitting on the sofa.

Chloe patted the open spot between her and Rory. "I saved you a seat," she said.

"Thanks! I'll be right back," I said.

After I served the punch, I put another batch of cookies in the microwave. They came out mushy. I cooked them another minute. They looked okay, but they tasted like watery hot chocolate with oatmeal lumps.

Buttons came over and sniffed around, but even she wouldn't eat them.

Angela ran in. "Are the cookies done yet?" she asked.

"Yes," I said, "but they taste terrible. I'll get some good cookies the next time I go to the store. Okay?"

"Okay," Angela said. "I don't want to watch the movie. Can I go outside?"

"Sure," I said. I gave her a drink and a snack plate, and she took Buttons outside to play.

I put veggies on a platter and chips into big bowls. I filled small bowls with dip. It took three trips to carry everything into the living room.

"Can I help you?" Rory asked on my second trip.

"No, thanks," I said. "I've got it."

When the snack bowls ran out, I hopped up to fill them. The movie ran for two hours. I sat down for twenty minutes. There was lots of room on our big sofa, especially since I didn't sit down much. Even so, Cameron sat so close to Chloe that their knees touched.

I was 100% positive
that he liked her as much as she liked him.

When the credits rolled, I hurried everyone out. I had a lot to do before Grandpa got home. Becca went to Claudia's house. Brad's dad gave Adam, Tommy, and Cameron a ride home. I was pretty sure they'd all had fun.

Chloe and I sat on the front steps while we waited for Rory's mom. Rory was playing keep-away with Angela and Buttons.

"It looked like you and Cameron had a good time," I said.

"I know I did," Chloe said. She blushed. "He put his arm around my shoulders."

"I noticed," I said.

"Cameron didn't want to come over until I told him you were going to be here," I said.

Chloe gasped. "Seriously?" she asked.

"Yeah," I said. "Believe me, Cameron is definitely into you."

Chloe was still grinning when she got into Mrs. Weber's car to leave.

Just call me Monica the Matchmaker!

Chapter Eight

Downhill
From There

When Angela and I walked back inside, I gasped.
The house was a disaster! Snack bowls, paper cups,
popcorn, and crumbs were scattered all over the living
room. There was dip spilled on the coffee table.

"What a mess!" Angela exclaimed.

"It's huge," I said.

I had to get it cleaned up before Grandpa got
home. He would never know I had eight kids in the
house — unless Angela tattled.

"Are you going to tell Grandpa I had people over?"
I asked.

"Nope," Angela said. She smiled. "I had fun."

"You look like it," I teased. Angela had dip in her hair and dirt on her knees. "You need a bath."

"After dinner," Angela said. She climbed onto a stool at the kitchen counter. "Mac and cheese, please."

I microwaved a frozen dinner for Angela, and then left to do more laundry. I folded the dry clothes, put the washed load in the dryer, and finally put the last load in the washer.

"I'm gonna take a bath now!" Angela hollered. I heard her go into the bathroom.

I grabbed a trash bag and started picking up paper cups and napkins. Then I stacked the dirty dishes in the sink. When Angela shouted for help, I ran into the bathroom.

"What's wrong?" I asked in a panic.

"My bubble bath is all gone," Angela cried.

"I can't buy more now," I said.

"Mom lets me use dish soap," Angela said.

"Okay, fine. I'll be right back," I said.

I had to keep Angela busy so I could work, so I was ready to do whatever she wanted. I filled the kitchen sink with water and added dish detergent. I left the party dishes to soak and took the bottle of soap to Angela. Then I went back to picking up trash.

Two minutes later, Angela shrieked again. Something was wrong.

I rushed back to the bathroom and stopped dead in the doorway. The bathtub was overflowing with bubbles. Angela was completely covered with white foamy suds.

"How much did you use?" I asked.

Angela held up the bottle. It was almost empty. "I'm sorry," she sobbed.

I had an even bigger mess to clean up now, but I didn't get mad. I just turned on the shower so Angela could rinse off.

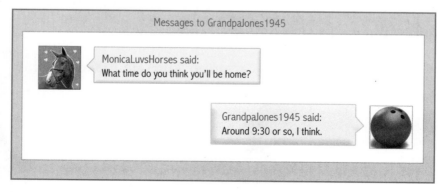

Messages to GrandpaJones1945

MonicaLuvsHorses said:
What time do you think you'll be home?

GrandpaJones1945 said:
Around 9:30 or so, I think.

Cleaning the bathroom took forever! There were bubbles all over the floor. I even saw some bubbles in the toilet. When I finally got the mess mopped up, I had a load of wet towels. I was too tired to do more laundry. I just left the towels in a basket.

It was only 8 o'clock. Angela didn't want to go to bed, and I didn't want to waste time fighting. I let her watch TV and got back to work. If I hurried, I could vacuum, do the dishes, and take out the trash before Grandpa got home at 9:30.

He came home at 8:19.

"You're not supposed to be here yet!" I exclaimed.

"Mr. Fenton's daughter got off work early," Grandpa said. He frowned. "Why is Angela still up? It's past her bedtime."

"She's been good, and I wanted to finish cleaning," I said. "She isn't watching anything scary."

"I should hope not," Grandpa said. He looked at the dirty dishes in the sink. "Is there something you want to tell me?"

"The dishes aren't done because Angela got soap bubbles all over the bathroom, and I had to clean it up," I explained.

"Time for bed, Angela," Grandpa said. "Turn off the TV, and I'll read you a story."

"Okay!" Angela said. She ran ahead into her room.

I followed Grandpa down the hall. He paused to look into the bathroom. It was sparkling clean, but he didn't say anything until he looked under Angela's bed.

"This isn't where your clothes and toys belong, Angela," Grandpa said. He lifted the bedspread so I could see. All of Angela's stuff was crammed underneath.

"I thought she put everything away," I said. "She told me she had."

Angela didn't want to be the only one in trouble. "Monica had a party with boys," Angela said.

"I know," Grandpa said.

My cheeks burned with embarrassment. "How did you know?" I ask.

"Party dishes in the sink and too many paper cups in the trash bag," Grandpa said. "You're grounded until your mom and Logan get home."

I had disappointed Grandpa again.

But secretly, I felt like it was worth it this time. I had fixed things between Cameron and Chloe.

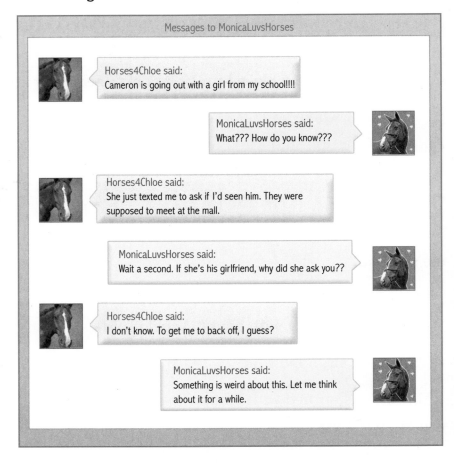

Messages to MonicaLuvsHorses

Horses4Chloe said:
Cameron is going out with a girl from my school!!!!

MonicaLuvsHorses said:
What??? How do you know???

Horses4Chloe said:
She just texted me to ask if I'd seen him. They were supposed to meet at the mall.

MonicaLuvsHorses said:
Wait a second. If she's his girlfriend, why did she ask you??

Horses4Chloe said:
I don't know. To get me to back off, I guess?

MonicaLuvsHorses said:
Something is weird about this. Let me think about it for a while.

Chapter Nine

Big Breaks

The next morning, Grandpa was already gone when I woke up. When he got home, I wanted everything to be perfect!

I got busy right away. Angela helped, too. She put all her stuff away while I cleaned the living room. I was ready to take a break when she wanted breakfast. She was still in her pajamas.

"Wash up and change clothes," I said. "I'll make fruit and waffles for brunch."

"Okay!" Angela said. She raced off.

I put two waffles into the toaster and sat down to think.

Chloe had been so happy the day before. Now she was crushed. Cameron couldn't be dating Katy. Could he? I had to find out. The truth might hurt, but it would be better for Chloe to know than for her to look like a fool.

Angela started shrieking before the waffles even popped up.

I ran to the bathroom. She was standing in a puddle of water. "What happened?" I asked.

"My socks fell in the toilet," Angela said.

I didn't see any socks. "Where are they?" I asked.

"I didn't want to stick my hand in so I flushed them and all this water came out." Angela said. "Are you mad?"

"No," I said. "Maybe I can fix it."

I used the plunger to push the socks through the pipes. When I flushed, the toilet overflowed. The socks were still stuck somewhere in there.

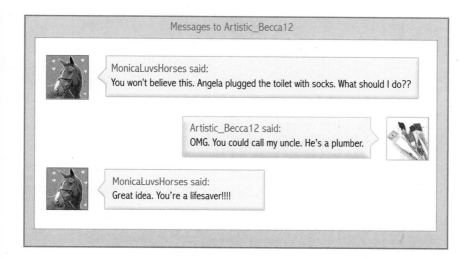

Messages to Artistic_Becca12

MonicaLuvsHorses said:
You won't believe this. Angela plugged the toilet with socks. What should I do??

Artistic_Becca12 said:
OMG. You could call my uncle. He's a plumber.

MonicaLuvsHorses said:
Great idea. You're a lifesaver!!!!

I called Becca's uncle's company, but he wasn't there. The guy who answered said it would cost $150 just to come out and look! I didn't have that much money. Not even close.

"Will Daddy be mad I broke the toilet?" Angela asked.

"It's not broken," I said. "It's just plugged up."

I didn't want to ask for help. But the toilet had to be working before Grandpa, Mom, and Logan got home. So I called Becca's dad.

Mr. McDougal came right over. He had to turn the water off to check the pipes.

I couldn't finish the laundry, so I finished making breakfast. I let Angela eat outside so she wouldn't bug me.

While I ate, my thoughts kept zipping back to the Cameron-Chloe-Katy love triangle.

Someone at Rock Creek Middle School probably knew what was going on. But the only Rock Creek kids I knew were the horse snobs from the barn and Rory.

I couldn't ask Megan or Lydia or Owen. They would make fun of Chloe. Rory wouldn't tease her. Still, she might be embarrassed if I told him what was going on.

Mr. McDougal came into the kitchen. "I have to get some tape and sealing glue at the hardware store," he told me. "I can't turn the water back on until I finish the job."

"Okay," I said.

As soon as Becca's dad left, I went right back to thinking about Chloe. I couldn't decide what to do. I was thinking so hard I didn't see Angela come back inside. I noticed her when she jumped in front me.

"The toilet's all apart!" Angela exclaimed.

"Use the one in Mom and Logan's room," I said. As she rushed out, I yelled, "But don't flush it!"

Rory was the only Rock Creek kid I could call. But first I had to think of a way to ask about Katy without telling him why I wanted to know.

Angela shrieked again.

This time, I walked. I knew I wouldn't find water all over the place. The water was turned off.

Instead, I found Angela staring at a broken bottle of perfume on the floor.

Elegance was Mom's favorite.

Chapter Ten

Simple
Solutions

🍀 "Now Traci will be mad at me too!" Angela whispered. She burst into tears.

"No, she won't," I said. "It was an accident. We'll buy a new bottle."

I left the mess and turned on the kitchen computer. Three stores in the mall had Elegance, but it cost $28.00.

"Is this an emergency?" Angela asked.

"Definitely," I said.

We only had $14.27 left of the $50 Mom had left for us. Angela broke the perfume, but I was in charge. It was my responsibility.

I had to use money from my riding-boot fund.

But I couldn't go to the mall. I was grounded. So I called Claudia.

"I'd love to go," Claudia said.

I sighed with relief.

"But I can't," Claudia said. "I still have homework."

I called Becca. She knocked on the door five minutes later.

"Are you grounded because of the party?" Becca asked. "We didn't mean to get you in trouble."

"It's not a big deal," I said. "I don't have time to go to the mall anyway. There's too much to do before my parents get home."

"I'm not grounded," Angela said.

Becca took the hint. "Can I take Angela?" she asked me.

"That would be great," I said.

"I have to get my Princess Patsy bag!" Angela yelled. She ran to her room.

I gave Becca the money. Then I asked for advice. "How would you find out if a friend's boyfriend likes someone else?" I asked.

Becca gasped. "What? Is Tommy —" she started.

I cut her off. "It's not about you," I said.

"Claudia?" Becca whispered.

"No!" I said, waving my hands. "Chloe. She got a text from the other girl."

"Maybe you should ask Cameron," Becca said.

Chapter Eleven

Priorities

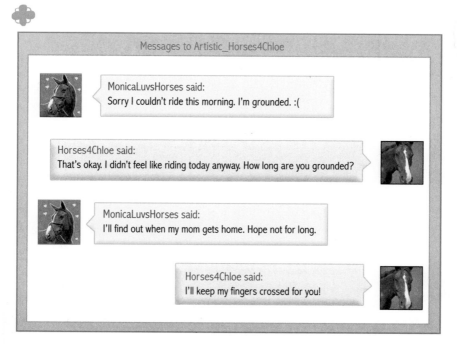

Messages to Artistic_Horses4Chloe

MonicaLuvsHorses said:
Sorry I couldn't ride this morning. I'm grounded. :(

Horses4Chloe said:
That's okay. I didn't feel like riding today anyway. How long are you grounded?

MonicaLuvsHorses said:
I'll find out when my mom gets home. Hope not for long.

Horses4Chloe said:
I'll keep my fingers crossed for you!

Chloe always felt like riding. It was what we both liked to do most in the world. **She was really**

depressed!

I had to do something.

Grandpa, Mom, and Logan wouldn't be home for hours. I decided that towels, dirty dishes, and a broken perfume bottle could wait.

Friends in trouble came first.

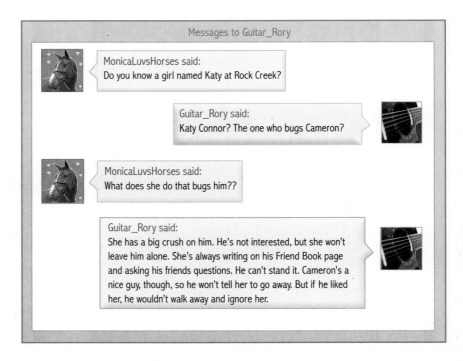

Messages to Guitar_Rory

MonicaLuvsHorses said:
Do you know a girl named Katy at Rock Creek?

Guitar_Rory said:
Katy Connor? The one who bugs Cameron?

MonicaLuvsHorses said:
What does she do that bugs him??

Guitar_Rory said:
She has a big crush on him. He's not interested, but she won't leave him alone. She's always writing on his Friend Book page and asking his friends questions. He can't stand it. Cameron's a nice guy, though, so he won't tell her to go away. But if he liked her, he wouldn't walk away and ignore her.

Horses4Chloe said:
I'm bored. Whatcha doing?

MonicaLuvsHorses said:
I've been thinking about that text Katy sent.

MonicaLuvsHorses said:
I don't think she and C. are together. She just wanted you to think they were.

Horses4Chloe said:
Why would she do that??

MonicaLuvsHorses said:
I don't know. So you'd get mad and break up with him?

Horses4Chloe said:
We're not exactly a real couple.

MonicaLuvsHorses said:
You might as well be. He obviously likes you.

Horses4Chloe said:
I thought so. But now I'm not so sure. I wish I knew the truth.

MonicaLuvsHorses said:
I know how you can find out. Next time you see them together, go over and say hi. I bet he walks away with you.

Horses4Chloe said:
I don't know. I'll think about it.

I couldn't finish my chores. I had to wait until Mr. McDougal put the toilet back together and turned the water back on. It was only five minutes past noon.

I had plenty of time.

And for the first time all weekend, I was Angela free!

I read my e-mail, wasted time online, and watched some silly videos. Then I heard the front door open. I thought it was Becca's dad.

It was Grandpa.

Chapter Twelve

The Right Thing
to Do

Grandpa was whistling when he walked into the house. He was in a good mood.

I wasn't. There was a broken toilet in one bathroom and a perfume puddle in the other. The breakfast dishes were still in the sink, and the wet towels were still in a basket.

Laundry was the only thing Grandpa had asked me to do, and I hadn't even done that.

I was so upset I wanted to cry.

But I didn't.

"How come you're home so early?" I asked.

"Doreen didn't have to work a double shift, and Mr. Fenton is feeling much better," Grandpa said. He opened the refrigerator and pulled out a soda. "Want one?"

I shook my head.

Grandpa sat on a stool and squinted at me. "Are you okay?"

I shook my head again. Then I started talking. "I wanted to get everything done before you and Logan and Mom got here," I said, "but Angela's socks got stuck in the toilet."

"How did that happen?" Grandpa asked.

"They fell in. Then she didn't want to put her hand in toilet water so she flushed them," I explained.

"Oh, no," Grandpa said.

"I couldn't get them out with a plunger," I went on, "so I called a plumber but it cost too much. Mr. McDougal came over to fix it but the toilet is all apart because he isn't back from the hardware store yet."

"I see," Grandpa said. He sipped his soda and nodded.

"Then Angela broke a bottle of Mom's perfume and I let her go to the mall with Becca to get more," I went on. "I thought I had plenty of time so I played on the computer instead of working."

"Sounds like you needed a break," Grandpa said.

"But I wanted the house to be perfect!" I said. I didn't mean to whine, but I was frustrated. "I had everything all planned out."

"Did you plan for flushed socks?" Grandpa asked.

"No!" I said. I laughed.

"Of course not," Grandpa said. "Things happen that we don't expect. That's just how life is. What matters is how you handle it."

"I couldn't handle it," I said. I felt so embarrassed.

I sighed. "I had to ask Becca's dad for help."

"I don't fix my car when it breaks down," Grandpa said. "I take it to a mechanic. Getting help was exactly the right thing to do."

Grandpa wasn't mad. That cheered me up a little, but I had still let him down.

"I'm sorry the house is such a mess," I said.

Grandpa smiled. "You'll do better next time," he said. Then he gave me a hug.

If there is a next time, I thought. Mom had only given me two rules, and I had broken both of them.

Grandpa helped Mr. McDougal put the toilet back together. I washed the wet towels and cleaned Mom's bathroom.

Then I did the hardest thing I had to do all weekend.

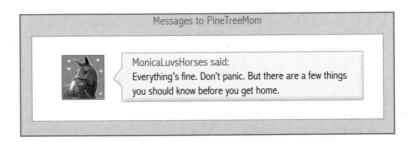

Monica's SECRET Blog

Sunday, 9:45 p.m.

Mom and Logan got back right before dinnertime. Luckily, Mom and I had been texting all afternoon, so she knew what had happened all weekend. I was shocked when she told me I wasn't in trouble! She said I did a good job taking care of Angela, and that the most important thing was that no one had gotten hurt. I do have to help with laundry for the rest of the week, but that's totally worth it for this weekend of drama.

I think maybe it was good for my relationship with Angela to spend so much time with her. It was definitely hard for both of us, but she liked being able to hang out with my friends, and I think I started to understand why she acts the way she does. I mean, she is just a little kid.

Mom said next time she and Logan go away, she'll think about leaving me in charge again. And she said if that goes well, maybe the NEXT time, Grandpa could go out of town too, and I could be in charge overnight. That would be amazing . . . but kind of a lot of responsibility! Well, I have plenty of time to get used to the idea.

I didn't tell her about the perfume. I didn't want her to be mad at Angela. I figure it doesn't make a big difference.

love,

Monica

 1 comment from Claudia: If your mom and dad go out of town, maybe I could come over and hang out. Sleepover!

Leave a comment:

Name (required)

FRIEND BOOK

Wall   Info   Photos   Notes

MONICA MURRAY

 AVATAR

SCREEN NAME: MonicaLuvsHorses

ABOUT ME:

View Photos of Me (100)

Edit My Profile

My Friends (236)

INFORMATION:

Relationship Status:
  Single

Astrological Sign:
  Taurus

Current City:
  Pine Tree

Family Members:
  Traci Gregory
  Logan Gregory
  Frank Jones
  Angela Gregory

Best Friends:
  Claudia Cortez
  Becca McDougal
  Chloe Granger
  Adam Locke
  Rory Weber
  Tommy Patterson
  Peter Wiggins

Activities: HORSEBACK RIDING!, hanging out with my friends, watching TV, listening to music, writing, shopping, sleeping in on weekends, swimming, watching movies . . . all the usual stuff

Favorite music: Tornado, Bad Dog, Haley Hover

Favorite books: A Tree Grows in Brooklyn, Harry Potter, Diary of Anne Frank, Phantom High

Favorite movies: Heartbreak High, Alien Hunter, Canyon Stallion

Favorite TV shows: Musical Idol, MyWorld, Boutique TV, Island

Fan of: Pine Tree Cougars, Rock Creek Stables, Pizza Palace, Red Brick Inn, K Brand Jeans, Miss Magazine, The Pinecone Press, Horse Newsletter Quarterly, Teen Scene, Boutique Magazine, Haley Hover

Groups: Peter for President!!!, Bring Back T-Shirt Tuesday, I Listen to WHCR In The Morning, Laughing Makes Everything Better!, I Have A Stepsister, Ms. Stark's Homeroom, Princess Patsy Is Annoying!, Haley Should Have Won on Musical Idol!, Pine Tree Eighth Grade, Mr. Monroe is the Best Science Teacher of All Time

Quotes: No hour of life is wasted that is spent in the saddle. ~Winston Churchill

A horse is worth more than riches.
~Spanish proverb

Mark my words

approve (uh-PROOV)—accept or think something is good

bribe (BRIBE)—money or a gift that you offer to a person to persuade them to do something for you

characters (KAR-ik-turz)—the people in a story, book, play, movie, or television show

depressed (di-PREST)—sad and gloomy

explanation (ek-spluh-NAY-shuhn)—a reason

grounded (GROUN-did)—not allowed to go out

ingredients (in-GREE-dee-uhnts)—items that something is made from

positive (POZ-uh-tiv)—sure or certain

reservations (rez-ur-VAY-shuhnz)—arrangements to save space for someone

responder (ri-SPON-dur)—the person whose job is to answer 911 calls

romantic (roh-MAN-tik)—to do with love

scratch (SKRATCH)—if something is made from scratch, it is homemade from the beginning

TEXT 911!

With your friends, help solve these problems.

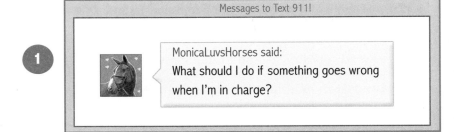

Messages to Text 911!

1

MonicaLuvsHorses said:
What should I do if something goes wrong when I'm in charge?

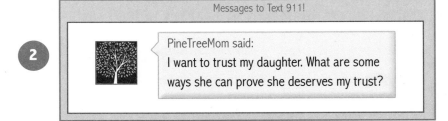

Messages to Text 911!

2

PineTreeMom said:
I want to trust my daughter. What are some ways she can prove she deserves my trust?

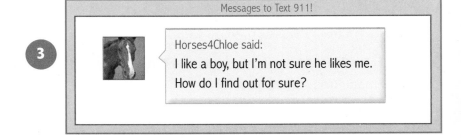

Messages to Text 911!

3

Horses4Chloe said:
I like a boy, but I'm not sure he likes me. How do I find out for sure?

You can write too.

Some people write in journals or diaries. I have a secret blog. Here are some writing prompts to help you write your own blog or diary entries.

1 For the first time, my mom and stepdad left me in charge. Write about a time you were given a new responsibility. What happened? How did you feel about it?

2 I really want Chloe and Cameron to become a real couple. Write about the most perfect couple you know. Who are they? What do they do that makes them seem perfect?

3 Sometimes my stepsister makes things go wrong. Write about your own siblings.

ABOUT THE AUTHOR: DIANA G. GALLAGHER

Just like Monica, Diana G. Gallagher has loved riding horses since she was a little girl. And like Becca, she is an artist. Like Claudia, she often babysits little kids — usually her grandchildren. Diana has wanted to be a writer since she was twelve, and she has written dozens of books, including the Claudia Cristina Cortez series. She lives in Florida.

CLAUDIA
CRISTINA CORTEZ
and
Monica

More stories about
Best Friends

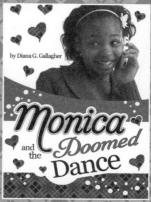

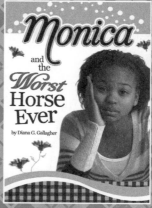

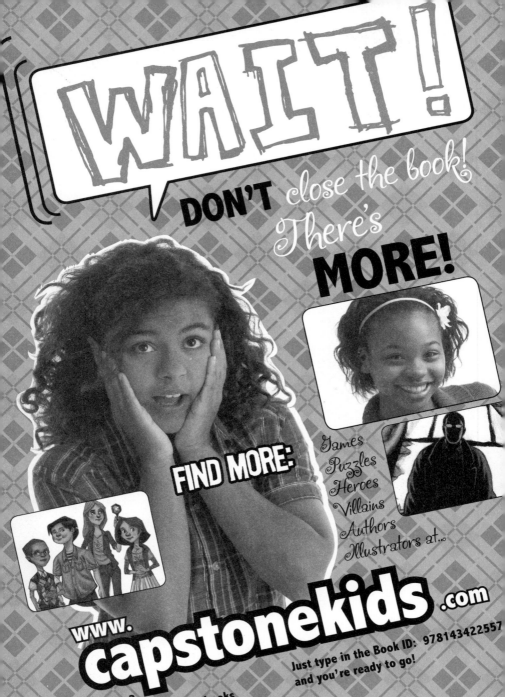